CYNTHIA LORD
Illustrated by ERIN MCGUIRE

Book  2

Shelter Pet Squad

Merlin

Scholastic Inc.

To Debbi

Text copyright © 2015 by Cynthia Lord
Illustrations © 2015 by Scholastic Inc.

All rights reserved. Published by Scholastic Inc., *Publishers since 1920.* SCHOLASTIC and associated logos are trademarks and/or registered trademarks of Scholastic Inc.

The publisher does not have any control over and does not assume any responsibility for author or third-party websites or their content.

This book is a work of fiction. Names, characters, places, and incidents are either the product of the author's imagination or are used fictitiously, and any resemblance to actual persons, living or dead, business establishments, events, or locales is entirely coincidental.

ISBN 978-0-545-63600-1

10 9 8 7 6 5 4 3 2 1   15 16 17 18 19

Printed in the U.S.A.   23
First printing 2015

The text was set in Janson MT.
Book design by Nina Goffi

Chapter 1

Shelter Pet Squad to the Rescue

Most Saturday mornings when I arrive at the Maplewood Animal Shelter to volunteer, things are calm and peaceful. Ms. Flores is behind the front counter, answering the phone and telling visitors about the animals. Ms. Kim and the rest of the Shelter Pet Squad kids are in the workroom, ready to make things to keep the animals busy and happy.

But not today! When I opened the front door, Ms. Flores was crawling on the floor, looking under the waiting-room chairs. Ms. Kim was searching through the dog-bed display.

"Quick, Suzannah! Close the door!" Ms. Flores said. "We can't let Merlin escape!"

She looked worried. I shut the door behind me as fast as I could. "Who's Merlin?" I asked. A hamster? A rabbit? A cat?

"A ferret!" Ms. Kim pulled the dog beds away from the wall and looked behind them. "His owner brought him to us a few days ago. This morning, he got out of his cage, and now we can't find him anywhere!"

The shelter takes care of stray and homeless pets until they get a new home. Ms. Kim and Ms. Flores work at the shelter, and there are five kids in Shelter Pet Squad: Jada, Matt,

Levi, Allie, and me. My best friend in the group is Jada. My least favorite kid is Allie, because she likes to get her own way every time.

"Merlin isn't in the cat room," Levi said, coming down the hallway with Matt. "We looked everywhere! Even under the cats' beds."

"What if one of the cats ate him?" Matt asked.

"Don't say that!" I heard Jada yell from the small-animal room.

"A cat wouldn't eat a ferret," Ms. Flores said. "But Merlin can get himself into places you wouldn't expect. Yesterday afternoon, I found him sleeping in the trash can near my desk."

"Good thing you didn't throw him away!" I peeked under a rack of books about pet care. I wasn't sure a ferret could even fit under there, though. I'd never seen a real ferret, only ferrets in pictures.

Under the books was just some dust — no animals.

Allie popped up from behind the front counter. "He's not in the trash can or the recycling bin."

"What does Merlin look like?" I asked, looking through a rack of leashes and collars.

"Like a weasel, but with a raccoon face." Matt made sideways *V*s with his fingers around his eyes, like a mask. "A weaselly thief!"

"You can say that again," Ms. Kim said. "On Thursday, I let him run around the waiting room so he could have some exercise. My coat was hanging on the back of my chair, and he stole my phone out of the pocket!"

"Maybe he wanted to call for pizza!" Jada said.

"Or he was calling his old owner to say 'Come back!'" Levi said.

Levi's comment made me sad. I don't like to think about people giving up animals, when I wish I could have one of my own. But we live in an apartment, and the landlord says "No pets."

Mom says that maybe someday we'll have our own house. Then we can have a real dog or cat or maybe even a ferret! But for now, the only pets I can have at home are toy stuffed animals. Bentley the dog and Whiskers the mouse are my favorites. I reached into my pocket to touch Whiskers's nose. I like to keep him with me, but he's a secret. None of the other kids bring stuffed animals with them.

"Hey!" Matt said, peering under the book-shelf. "Look at this!"

We all rushed over. "Did you find him?" Allie asked.

"No. I found a quarter!"

We sighed.

"Ferrets can climb," Ms. Flores said. "So we need to look *up*, too."

I looked around, down, and up. Where would a ferret go? Maybe behind the bags of dog food on the donation shelf? As I walked over to check, I stopped to pat Shadow, one of the waiting-room cats, asleep in a chair. Some-one had left a coat and a purse hanging on the back of the chair.

The coat didn't look lumpy, but I patted it

down just in case. It was all squishy. Nothing was hiding there. Then, the purse moved.

A car horn started blaring from the parking lot: *BEEP, BEEP, BEEP!*

Matt ran to the window. "Ms. Kim, that's your car!"

BEEP, BEEP, BEEP!

Usually, I wouldn't touch a purse that wasn't mine, but a purse can't move on its own. I lifted the purse's front flap.

I saw two little white ears.

A pink nose poked out.

A tan face appeared, with a mask of dark brown fur surrounding shiny black eyes. And a mouth was clutching the remote for a set of car keys.

"I found him!" I said.

Chapter 2

Appearing and Disappearing

BEEP! BEEP! BEEP! Ms. Kim's car horn was still blaring from the parking lot.

"Is this your purse?" I asked. "Because Merlin is inside!"

Ms. Kim laughed. "Yes. Thank you, Suzannah! When I arrived, Ms. Flores told me that Merlin was missing. So I just dropped my coat and purse on that chair to start looking. He must've snuck in there while I was hunting for him."

Before she could reach him, Merlin jumped

out. He looked like a tan-and-brown weasel. He had a funny, bouncy run, with his back high in the air. In his mouth, he clutched the car remote and Ms. Kim's keys.

BEEP, BEEP, BEEP!

"There he goes!" I hurried after him.

"Wow, he's fast!" Matt said.

Merlin zipped around the corner of the counter and under Ms. Flores's desk.

"Now we've got him!" I dropped to my hands and knees to look under the desk. I expected to see Merlin in a dark corner, but the only thing under the desk was a paper clip. "He's gone again!"

"Merlin is a perfect name for him," Matt said. "In the King Arthur stories, Merlin was a wizard. Our Merlin can appear and disappear, too!"

Ms. Flores slowly pulled open the bottom desk drawer. There was Merlin sitting on some folders and papers. There were other things in the drawer, too.

A little plastic cat ball with a jingle bell inside.

A stuffed toy hedgehog.

A plastic bag.

A few shiny dog tags from the display.

A washcloth.

A little fold-up umbrella.

And Ms. Kim's keys.

"So *that's* where my umbrella went!" Ms. Flores picked up Merlin with one hand around his back and the other hand supporting his hind legs. Ms. Kim wiggled her car keys out of his mouth and pushed the button on the remote to stop the car horn from honking. "Merlin, we found your secret robber's den!"

"We'll have to find a safer place to keep the plastic bags," Ms. Flores said. "Thank goodness he didn't chew this one. It could've hurt him if he'd swallowed any plastic." She sighed. "We need to do more ferret-proofing. Ferrets need time out of their cages every day for

exercise. Merlin needs a safe place to play and explore where he can't get into trouble or hurt himself."

"Or steal things!" Jada added.

Merlin made a low, chuckling, *uh-uh-uh-uh* sound.

"Is he laughing?" Allie asked.

"You could say that." Ms. Kim scratched Merlin's head. "That's called dooking. Ferrets make that sound when they're happy. He liked playing chase with us. He thought that was a fun game."

"We could help you ferret-proof," I said. "What do we need to do?"

"I'm not sure," said Ms. Flores. "We don't get many ferrets at the shelter. So I need to do some research. I borrowed some ferret books from another shelter, but we've been so busy getting ready for the Make-A-Match-A-Thon that I haven't had a chance to read them yet."

"Make-A-Match-A-Thon? What is that?" Allie asked.

Ms. Kim gave us a wide smile. "I've been excited to tell you about it! The Make-A-

Match-A-Thon is a big adoption event at the mall next Saturday. Lots of animal shelters will be there, showing their animals to people who might like to adopt them," she explained. "And I was hoping you all might like to come! You could show visitors how to make fun things for the animals. What do you think, Shelter Pet Squad?"

"Yes!" Levi said. "I bet I can go!"

"Me, too!" I said.

Matt grinned. "Me three!"

"I can't wait!" said Allie, clapping her hands.

"Maybe we could help you tell people about the animals, too!" Jada said.

"That would be wonderful," Ms. Kim replied. "We're planning to bring some of our cats and dogs and Gizmo, a hamster that came in this week. But we haven't decided if we should bring Merlin or not."

"Why?" I asked. "He's so cute. People will love him."

"That's the problem," Ms. Flores said. "Ferrets *are* cute, but ferret owners need to understand their pets. Merlin's first owner bought him at a pet store, and she didn't know important things about ferrets."

"Like what?" Allie asked.

"Merlin's first owner didn't know that ferrets like small, cozy spaces," Ms. Flores said. "Merlin chewed a hole under her couch and crawled inside and got stuck. She had to rip her couch to get Merlin out. The lady didn't know that ferrets like to take things, either.

Merlin took her watch off her dresser and dropped it down a heating vent. She had to hire someone to take the vent apart to get her watch back. And ferrets have a smell that she didn't like."

"That's mean!" I said. "That's not Merlin's fault."

Ms. Flores cuddled him. "I tried to help the lady understand that Merlin was just being a ferret. But she said a ferret was too much work for her, and she decided to give Merlin away."

"So I'm afraid if we bring Merlin with us to the Make-A-Match-A-Thon, the same thing could happen again," Ms. Kim said. "Someone who isn't ready for a ferret might be tempted to adopt him on the spot."

"But if you leave him behind, he might miss

out on his chance to be adopted by the *right* person," Levi said.

"Yes!" I agreed. "What if the right person comes and he's not there?"

Merlin dooked again, nuzzling under Ms. Flores's chin.

"He's tired out," Jada said.

"I'm tired, too!" Matt said. "I can see how his first owner thought he was a lot of work."

I scowled. Merlin couldn't help that! "People should have to pass a test to prove they *know* about ferrets before they can take one home," I said.

Levi looked at me. "That's a great idea, Suzannah. We can make a ferret quiz and bring it to the Make-A-Match-A-Thon! We won't let anyone adopt Merlin who doesn't pass the test."

Ms. Kim smiled. "What a wonderful plan! Let's bring the ferret books back to the workroom with us. We can look at the information in the books to find some good questions to ask."

Allie wrinkled her nose. "That sounds like homework."

"It will be worth it if we find Merlin a home," Jada said. "I like Suzannah's idea."

I felt proud that it was *my* idea that would help Merlin find a new family. A family that wouldn't adopt him just because he was cute. Or be disappointed when he took things or crawled into small, cozy spaces.

A family that would love him — just as he was.

A home that needed a ferret.

Chapter 3

The Hard Part

There are many good parts about being in Shelter Pet Squad.

I like to make things for the dogs.

The cats are fun to play with and pat.

I love giving treats to the small animals.

It's exciting to be part of a club.

But there's one hard part about Shelter Pet Squad.

I'm the youngest.

Levi is in sixth grade, Matt's in fifth grade,

Allie and Jada are in third grade, and I'm in second. Sometimes being the youngest doesn't matter. But sometimes it does.

Allie and Jada ride their bikes to the shelter together. Mom says I'm too young to do that, though. So she drives me, and I'm usually last to get there.

I'm a good reader in my class at school, but I could see that Ms. Flores's ferret books were for grown-ups. Books with long words and small print. I was scared that I wouldn't be able to read them. As we walked to the workroom, I reached into my pocket to touch Whiskers. Funny how just having a friend can make you feel twice as brave as you are by yourself.

As we sat around the table, Matt picked up one of the big books about ferrets. "We'll use this book to get some ideas." He turned to the Table of Contents. "Here are the chapter subjects: food, health, housing, grooming, behavior, and toys. Wow, that's a lot to learn about."

"We can each learn about one category," Levi said. "And report on it next week."

"I'll do toys!" I said quickly. That sounded fun.

Allie huffed. "I wanted toys!"

Levi shook his head. "Suzannah called it. I'll take behavior."

Allie hopped out of her chair to look at the Table of Contents. I think she was afraid to lose another favorite if she didn't hurry. "I'll do housing. That's a cage, right?"

"Read and find out!" Matt said. "I'll do

grooming. How to keep your ferret looking *fabulous*!"

"That leaves food and health," Jada said. "I'll do food."

"And I'll do health," Ms. Kim said.

When Matt asked who wanted to take a book home, I took the biggest one. The book was really heavy, but I didn't want to look like a baby. I turned to the back and saw the book had three hundred pages. That was bad news.

I flipped through a few pages. There were lots of photos. Photos were good news.

"So what time is the Make-A-Match-A-Thon next week?" Jada asked. "I'll have to tell my mom."

"And I need to put it on our calendar," Matt

said. "My dad says, 'If it's not on the calendar, it doesn't happen!'"

"I can't remember the exact times," Ms. Kim said, opening the supply cupboard. "Levi, would you look? The announcement is on the table." As she took a package of small white socks from the cupboard, I wondered what we were making today. Treat puzzles for the dogs? Toys for the cats?

Levi picked up the paper. "It says one to three o'clock," he said. "Uh-oh."

Ms. Kim turned around. "What's the matter?"

"It says any participating kids must be at least eight years old. And anyone under eighteen has to be directly supervised by an adult," he said.

"That's no problem," Ms. Kim said. "I'll be there to supervise you all."

Levi glanced at me.

I swallowed hard. "I'm only seven. But I'm seven *and a half.*" Which wasn't really true, but I figured anything after my birthday counted as a half.

"If Suzannah can't do it, does that mean *none* of us can do it?" Allie asked, looking at me.

I didn't like how fast Allie was ready to leave me out. I was part of Shelter Pet Squad, too!

"I'll call the person in charge and explain," Ms. Kim said. "Don't worry, Suzannah. I'm sure it'll be okay."

I swallowed hard. It *had* to be okay. I didn't want to be only kid who couldn't go!

Ms. Kim put a pile of little socks, empty toilet-paper tubes, spoons, markers, and several bags of catnip on the table. "Today, we're making Catnip Critters for our shelter cats."

"My two cats at home love catnip," Matt said. "Charlotte and Stuart Little always act silly when we give it to them. I call it crazy nip."

"Charlotte and Stuart Little?" Levi asked. "You have a cat named after a spider? And another named after a mouse? That's kind of goofy, Matt."

Matt shrugged. "*Stuart Little* and *Charlotte's Web* were my favorite books when I was a little kid."

A little kid? I glanced sideways at Matt. I still liked those books.

"Take a sock and put the toilet-paper tube inside. Using the spoon, fill the toe with catnip," Ms. Kim explained. "When you've packed it in there, we'll remove the tube and tie the open end of the sock in a knot to keep the catnip inside. Then you can use the nontoxic markers to draw a face and add some details to make your toy look like an animal. I thought this could be a fun project for you to make with the kids who come to the Make-A-Match-A-Thon next week."

"This *will* be fun!" Jada said, grabbing a sock.

The catnip was messy and smelled funny,

but I knew the cats would love these toys. When the toe of my sock was full of catnip, I took out the toilet-paper tube and knotted the sock.

"It looks like a fish," Matt said. "So mine will be a shark!"

"I'm making a mouse," said Jada. "What are you making, Suzannah?"

"A ferret." I picked up the brown marker. "Just like Merlin."

As I drew a little mask on the toe of my sock, I thought about the ferret quiz and finding Merlin a home.

So what if the book about ferrets was really big? I only had to read about toys.

Really, how hard could it be?

Chapter 4

Fun with Your Ferret

At home the next day, I carried two of my stuffed animals to my bed so they could look at the big ferret book with me. Bentley, my favorite dog, sat on my lap. Whiskers was tucked into the front of my shirt, just peeking out.

The book had lots of pages and the print was very small. I took a deep breath to pull in some courage. My teacher says that when you're reading and come to a word that you

don't know, there are things you can do that'll help.

Try sounding it out.

Read the sentence and see what makes sense.

If there's a picture, maybe it will give you a clue.

I looked at the table of contents. Chapter 6 was called "Fun with Your Ferret." That sounded like it might talk about toys, and all those words were easy.

Fun. With. Your. Ferret. I didn't even have to sound those out.

Chapter 6 started on page 57. I lifted the bottom corners of the pages until I found it. On that page was a super-cute photo of a ferret playing with a ball. He had a fur mask around his eyes, just like Merlin.

I smiled wider as I turned the pages. Some ferrets were tan-and-brown. Some were white. A few were almost all black. They were playing with balls, climbing through big tubes, crawling in and out of piles of blankets, and carrying little stuffed animals in their mouths.

"Don't worry, Whiskers," I said, patting his tiny ears. "You'll never be a ferret toy."

I hopped off my bed and found some paper and a pencil. I needed to write down the important things.

Ferrets like lots of toys to play with. They like balls, tubes and tunnels, little animals (stuffed, not real), and blanket piles to climb in.

My writing looked messy, but this was just my first draft. I could write it again neater before I brought my notes to the shelter.

Returning to my bed, I put Bentley in my lap again. On the next page of the book, one ferret was digging in a garden. Another was digging in the snow. Under the photos, it said that sometimes they dig in plant pots, too. I picked up my pencil.

Ferrets love to dig! So watch out for your plants!

A brown ferret had his paws in a tub of

water. In the water, a toy boat bobbed beside a rubber duckie.

Ferrets like tub toys, too!

My favorite photo showed ferrets playing with a cardboard box. Someone had cut a hole in the side of a box, and a little white ferret face was peeking out.

Ferrets enjoy boxes.

In other photos, ferrets played with paper bags and baby rattles. One caption said that ferrets love to play chase.

They also love bags, rattles, and chasing things — or other ferrets.

Just looking at the photos and reading the captions was giving me lots of facts about ferret toys. I couldn't wait to tell the other kids the cool things I'd found out. They would be amazed that the youngest kid had read the hardest book! They didn't need to know that I had mostly looked at the pictures.

I told Mom and Dad about the Make-A-Match-A-Thon and how we were going to find the right home for Merlin. "We're making a quiz, and anyone who wants to adopt him will have to know the answers. I read all about toys," I explained.

When Saturday finally came, I was so excited that I didn't even care that I was the last kid there. I skipped through the shelter parking lot, carrying the book about ferrets with my notes.

But when I stepped inside, Ms. Kim was waiting with a sad look on her face.

"I'm sorry, Suzannah," she said.

That's how I knew something was wrong.

Chapter 5

A Bad Surprise

Ms. Kim put her arm around me. "Suzannah, I called the organizers of the Make-A-Match-A-Thon. I explained that you were an important member of our Shelter Pet Squad and you were almost eight years old but not quite. They said the age rule was important to their insurance company. Everyone at our booth has to be at least eight years old."

She looked at Mom. "Is there any chance

you could come? The organizers said Suzannah could participate if you're with us."

That wouldn't be the same at all. Everything in me slumped. My hands let go of the heavy ferret book, and it fell right on my big toe. Tears hopped into my eyes.

"Are you okay, Suzannah?" Jada looked sorry for me.

Everyone thought my tears were from toe pain. My foot did hurt, but being left out hurt worse. I looked down at a box full of leashes and cat toys ready to go to the Make-A-Match-A-Thon.

"I did have some more errands I was going to run today," Mom said to me. "But I could try to rearrange those while you're in your meeting. Do you still want to go?"

The angry part of me wanted to say, *No!* and *Never mind!* But I also wanted to see Merlin get adopted. "I don't know," I finally said. "I'll think about it."

"Okay, I'll be back at the regular time to get you," Mom said. "You can tell me then."

Carrying the ferret book to the workroom,

I felt like an ant — one minute I was running around being happy and suddenly a big foot came and stomped me flat.

"It's a dumb rule," Levi said, sitting beside me at the worktable. "You're very mature for your age."

I think he was trying to make me feel better, but he just sounded like a grown-up, too.

Ms. Kim took out a stack of small posters. Each one had the logo for Maplewood Animal Shelter and a slogan.

IT'S COOL TO ADOPT!

MY FOREVER HOME.

IT WAS LOVE AT FIRST SIGHT.

I'M HEADING HOME!

MY NEW FAMILY.

NEW BEST FRIENDS.

"Today's project will be to decorate these signs," Ms. Kim said. "We'd like to take a photo of everyone who adopts an animal today. I thought they could hold one of these signs. You can make it look special with some drawings or a colorful border or whatever you'd like."

I reached into the pile and picked the sign that said, IT WAS LOVE AT FIRST SIGHT. I'm not great at drawing animals, but I'm good at drawing hearts.

Jada picked I'M HEADING HOME! "What are you going to draw?" she asked me.

I chose a red marker. "I'm drawing a border of hearts all around the edges."

"Nice!" Jada said. "Do you mind if I put a border of little houses around mine, too?"

"Sure." I felt a little better that Jada liked my idea so much that she asked to copy it.

"I'm going to imagine that an animal lives in every one of these," Jada said, drawing little blue houses. "This one is for Gizmo the hamster. This one is for Peter the cat. Here's one for Merlin."

"Hey, guys, while we're working on our signs, why don't we make the ferret quiz?" Levi said, pulling out his notebook. "You can tell me your facts and I'll write them into questions."

I plopped the big ferret book on the table next to my sign. My notes were sticking out of the top. I wanted everyone to see I was ready for my turn.

"Maybe the first question should be 'Have you had a ferret before?'" Ms. Kim said, coloring the puppy face she had drawn on NEW BEST FRIENDS. "An experienced owner would be wonderful for Merlin."

Levi nodded. "That owner would know what he was getting into."

"And he wouldn't get mad when Merlin acted like a ferret," Matt said, drawing a cat face on IT'S COOL TO ADOPT!

"I think the next questions should be about food," Jada said, taking out her notes. "Ferrets are obligate carnivores."

I was glad I hadn't picked food. Those were really big words. I nodded and drew more hearts, pretending I knew what *obli-something* meant.

"I had to look that up," Jada said. "It means that ferrets need meat in their diets to be healthy. They can eat other things, but meat is how they get most of their nutrients. They also need fresh water every day. Ferrets can have occasional treats, like eggs or bites of raw chicken, beef, pork, or fish."

I fingered the edge of my notes. I was excited for my turn.

"Are there any foods that ferrets *can't* have?" Allie asked.

"Ferrets can get sick if you feed them chocolate or drinks with caffeine, like coffee,"

Jada explained. "It also said to avoid sugary treats."

"Those are good facts, but a quiz needs questions," said Levi. "How about 'What are some good foods and good drinks for ferrets?' and 'What would you give Merlin for a treat?'"

"Be sure you put the answers next to the questions," said Matt. "So we can check the person's answers when we give them the quiz."

When Levi finished writing, I hoped he'd ask about toys, but he took out his own notes. "I read about behavior. Ferrets are smart and playful. Someone needs to be watching a ferret when he's out of his cage. Otherwise he could get hurt or make a mess. Sometimes ferrets nip."

Ms. Kim nodded. "Just like when puppies or kittens put their teeth on you. It's playful, not trying to hurt."

"Ferrets love to take things and hide them, as we all know," Levi said. "They also like to dig."

"There's a photo in my book of a ferret digging in a plant pot!" I found the photo and showed everyone.

"What a mess!" Matt said.

"Maybe we should ask people if they have houseplants?" suggested Jada. "If they say yes, we can warn them about the digging."

Most of the questions we came up with about behavior began with "Will you get mad if . . ." For example: "Will you get mad if your ferret tips over his food bowl or water dish?" and "Will you get mad if your ferret nips you?"

Then Allie told us about housing. I tried hard to be patient for my turn.

"A ferret cage or habitat shouldn't be in direct sunlight or anywhere that the ferret could feel cold," Allie said. "They need a large habitat with different levels to climb on with a hammock, a hiding place, a litter box, and toys. There should be bedding material like shredded paper or wood shavings, but cedar shavings are harmful to ferrets."

"Wow, there's a lot to learn," said Levi, writing quickly.

"Yes," Ms. Kim said. "And it's really important to know as much as you can before you bring an animal home. As you can see, an animal could get sick or hurt if you make a mistake. We were very lucky on the day that Merlin escaped."

For health, Ms. Kim told us how a sick ferret might lose weight or lose his fur. "A healthy ferret sleeps a lot — up to eighteen to twenty hours every day," she said. "When he's awake, he should be playful and alert. He'll eat and drink regularly and have bright eyes and a shiny coat."

"I can tell you how to keep that coat shiny!" said Matt. "Because I wrote facts about how to keep your ferret looking fit, fine, and fabulous!"

"Wait until I turn those into questions!" Levi said, writing quickly. "Okay, go!"

I sighed as Matt told us ferrets needed a bath

at least once a month and how often to clean their ears and cut their nails and brush their fur.

Finally, it was my turn! I tingled with excitement to be the expert. "Ferrets like lots of toys to play with," I read from my notes. "They like balls, tubes and tunnels, little animals (stuffed, not real), and blanket piles to climb in. Ferrets love to dig! So watch out for your plants! Ferrets like tub toys, too! Ferrets enjoy boxes. They also love bags, rattles, and chasing things — or other ferrets."

"Wonderful job!" Ms. Kim said.

"Yes, that's great information," Levi said.

I beamed and handed Levi my notes. As he wrote questions for toys, I finished the last few hearts on my border. They were all red, but some were a little lopsided. It didn't look as perfect as I had imagined it.

Ms. Flores poked her head in the workroom. "Our volunteers have loaded up the van. We're taking as many cages and animals as we can safely fit in there," she said. "Ms. Kim, I'm going to the mall with them. Can you bring the kids with you when you're ready?"

No one said, "Except Suzannah," but I was thinking it.

"We just need to finish our signs and then pack up the activities that we're bringing to show the visitors." Ms. Kim looked at me kindly. "Suzannah, I hope you'll come with your mom."

"Yes, please come! It won't be the same without you," Jada said.

I shrugged. I wanted to go, but I also wanted to stay mad. I still didn't think it was fair.

"Suzannah, maybe you could go down to the cat room and choose some toys for Merlin?" Ms. Kim suggested. "He'll enjoy having some things to play with while he's in his pen at the mall."

That felt like one more thing I was doing by myself. But I wanted Merlin to have toys. "How many should I pick?"

"How about five little ones? That sounds about right," Ms. Kim said.

In the cat room, seven older cats were staying behind. Buster, a gray striped cat, rubbed the side of his face against my pant leg. I ran my hand down his back. "I'm sorry you didn't get picked to go today," I told him.

Buster purred beside me as I opened the toy box and chose two balls and three little stuffed toys for Merlin. Then I chose toys for the cats staying behind.

"Even though you aren't going to the Make-A-Match-A-Thon, you can still have some fun," I said to Buster. "Right?"

I put the cats' toys in funny places for them to find and play with. I squeezed Catnip Critters into the stacks of blankets, just peeking out. I hung a rope toy on the doorknob. I put balls on the different platforms of the cat towers.

Buster went to the Catnip Critter I had made. He pulled on it with his teeth until it popped out of the blankets. Then he rolled onto his back, clutching it with his claws. Seeing the little ferret face I had drawn made me smile a little. It looked like Merlin was playing with Buster.

Buster was having fun, even though he wasn't going to the mall with the younger cats. He wasn't moping around feeling sorry for himself. And right then, I knew my decision.

Chapter 6

The Make-A-Match-A-Thon

The middle of the mall looked like a big animal fair. Many animal organizations and businesses were there: shelters, companies that make pet toys and treats, dog trainers, and groomers. There were lots of tables and banners and balloons. Dogs and cats peeked out of cages. There were pens with puppies and kittens for people to hold. All around us, there were people talking and dogs barking.

"The Make-A-Match-A-Thon is a Make-

A-*Noise*-A-Thon," I told Mom as we walked past other organizations.

"There's our group!" Mom said.

Ms. Flores was standing behind a long table covered with a tablecloth that said, MAPLEWOOD ANIMAL SHELTER. On our table were leashes and collars for sale, brochures, and clipboards with adoption forms. Beside Ms. Flores, a woman was writing on a form, and a boy held Coco, a fuzzy little brown dog that had been at the shelter ever since I started volunteering two months ago. The boy held Coco against his shoulder, and she licked his ear.

I was so happy for Coco that I smiled my first one-hundred-percent-happy smile since Ms. Kim told me seven was too young to come to the Make-A-Match-A-Thon by myself.

"I'm so glad you're here, Suzannah!" she said, coming over to me. "It wouldn't be Shelter Pet Squad without you." She handed me my Shelter Pet Squad name tag.

"Is Coco getting adopted?" I asked, putting on my name tag. The boy looked like he loved Coco already.

Ms. Kim grinned. "Yes! Let's show her new family our signs."

Mom and I followed Ms. Kim. On the way, I waved to Jada and Allie showing some kids how to make Catnip Critters at another table.

"Thank you for adopting!" Ms. Kim said to the woman and the boy. "When you're done with the paperwork, we'd like to take your photo with Coco, if that's okay? Suzannah will show you some signs you can choose from."

I flipped through the signs so the boy could pick. "I made this one," I said when I got to mine.

"I'll choose that one," the boy said. "It really *was* love at first sight for us."

"Just take the sign over to the boy in the blue T-shirt. His name is Matt," Ms. Kim said. "He'll take your photo."

As Matt took their photo, the boy rested his cheek on Coco's head. Her tail was wagging and she looked so happy. I wished someone would love Merlin like that, too.

"Has anyone taken the ferret quiz?" I asked Ms. Kim.

"Not yet," she said. "Lots of people have been interested in Merlin, but no one has been ready to adopt him. Would you like to see him?

He's in a pen down at the end. And the ferret quiz is tucked in back."

As Mom and I walked past the cages, I told her about the animals. "This big dog is named Texas. He likes to bark. The yellow cat that's sleeping is Marmalade. This white cat is Peter. One time, he sat on my lap so long that my leg fell asleep. And here's Merlin."

His pen was a tall circular fence. Inside the pen was a litter box, a pet bed, food, water, a plastic igloo to hide in, and the toys I'd chosen. A lady with short hair was standing outside the pen, reaching down to scratch Merlin's back. He swung his head around and grabbed the edge of the lady's coat sleeve in his teeth, ready to wrestle.

"Hi," I said to the lady. "Just to warn you —

sometimes ferrets nip, but it's just their way of playing."

"Oh, I know," she said, gently wrestling with him. "I've had a ferret before."

"You have?" My eyes flew wide open. Here was Merlin's chance! "He's a great ferret! His name is Merlin. His first owner bought him at a pet store but then got mad when he chewed a hole in her couch and dropped her watch down a heating vent, and —"

I swallowed the rest of what I was going to say. I didn't want her to think he was a troublemaker.

But the lady smiled. "My ferret, Mitzi, once emptied an entire bag of flour all over my kitchen floor. She had a great time rolling in it. She was such a funny little rascal."

Merlin jumped onto the woman's coat sleeve. She scooped him up, one hand under his hind legs and one around his back. She smiled at him, but her eyes were sad. "Mitzi died a few months ago."

"I'm so sorry," Mom said, and the lady smiled. I was glad Mom knew what to say.

"Thank you," the lady said. "Mitzi was more than a pet. She was a member of my family." She set Merlin gently back in his pen. "I was just at the mall shopping, but when I saw him, I had to come over."

"He's a fun ferret." I reached down to pick up the ferret quiz from behind Merlin's pen. I was pretty sure the lady would know all the answers, but I was still going to ask the questions. "And he already likes you."

She sighed. "He's wonderful, but I can't imagine having another ferret. No other ferret would be Mitzi."

My heart dropped. I couldn't believe it. I'd found a great person to adopt Merlin, but she didn't want him. I looked down at the quiz in my hands. "Do you know *anyone* looking for a ferret? We really want to find him a good home."

"I do know some other ferret owners. I'll tell them about Merlin. They'll help spread the word." The lady reached down to pat Merlin again. He put his nose in the sleeve of her coat.

Then all I saw was his tail!

"Oh! My goodness!" she said, laughing.

Then even his tail disappeared. A big lump was moving up inside the lady's coat sleeve.

Mom helped her unbutton her coat and, suddenly, there was Merlin! Right at the woman's shoulder, peeking out from inside her sleeve.

"You're a little rascal, too!" the lady said.

"Merlin is always appearing and disappearing," I told her.

She held him gently and placed him back in his pen. "He's a great ferret. He'll make someone very happy. I'll do what I can to help you."

Merlin and I both watched the lady until she was gone. I tried to interest him in the toys I'd picked for him, but he didn't want to play. He just lay down and watched the people walk by.

"He's tired," Mom said. "It must be confusing for him to be here with all this activity."

All afternoon, people came by to see Merlin. They loved to watch him and play with him, but not one person got past the "behavior" part of the quiz before deciding they wanted a cat or a dog. *But cats and dogs are work, too!* I wanted to tell them.

At three o'clock, Ms. Flores folded the tablecloth and packed up the leftover brochures. Jada and Allie cleared away the catnip, cardboard tubes, spoons, socks, and markers.

Levi and Matt took down the balloons and stacked the signs.

I stayed with Merlin until Ms. Flores put him in a pet carrier to take him to the van. Many animals had found homes today, but Merlin was going back to the shelter.

"Shelter Pet Squad, gather around!" Ms. Kim said. "I have an idea for our meeting next week. Let's make something fun for Merlin to cheer him up. Suzannah, since you read about ferret toys, would you like to choose our project?"

"But what if Merlin gets adopted before next week?" Allie asked.

"I hope that happens!" Ms. Kim said. "If it does, we can always give the toys to Merlin's new owner. What do you think, Suzannah?

Do you want to be in charge of our meeting next week?"

I grinned. "Yes!"

Ms. Kim said the Make-A-Match-A-Thon was a big success. Twenty-two animals from our shelter were adopted, including Marmalade, Peter, Texas, and Coco. Even the little hamster, Gizmo, found a new home with a girl and her dad.

We had lots of photos for the shelter website of people holding our signs and their new pets.

Many people chose IT WAS LOVE AT FIRST SIGHT.

But no one chose Merlin.

Chapter 7

Good Surprises

For the next few days, I thought hard about what fun toy to make for Merlin at Shelter Pet Squad. The shelter already had some toys.

There were lots of balls.

Merlin had plenty of small stuffed animals.

He had little squeaky toys.

I read through my notes, looking for ideas: *Ferrets like lots of toys to play with. They like balls, tubes and tunnels, little animals (stuffed, not real), and blanket piles to climb in. Ferrets love to dig! So watch out for your plants! Ferrets like tub toys, too! Ferrets enjoy boxes. They also love bags, rattles, and chasing things — or other ferrets.*

A bin of dirt to dig in would be too messy.

I couldn't think of any bath toys to make.

Ferrets enjoy boxes. I thought about that photo I'd seen of a ferret peeking out of a box. Maybe we could make some cardboard-box houses for Merlin? We could cut doors and windows for him to climb in and out. Maybe there could be a paper-towel-tube chimney at the top! Then he'd have both a box and a tunnel — two things that ferrets like!

If we each made him a house, then Ms. Flores and Ms. Kim could put out a different one every day. That way, he wouldn't get bored with the same one all the time. And if he chewed on them, it wouldn't matter, because they were just boxes.

"I need five medium-size boxes," I said to Mom and Dad that night at supper. "One for each kid in Shelter Pet Squad."

"I think I can bring some home from work," Dad said. "About how big do you need?"

"Ferret size!" I said, holding my hands up to show him.

On Saturday, I was so excited to show the kids my idea that I hurried through the shelter parking lot with two boxes stacked in my arms. I could barely see over them! Mom helped by carrying the rest of the boxes and a bunch of paper-towel tubes.

"Watch out, Suzannah," she said. "There's something on the doorstep."

On the front step of the shelter was a little plastic bag of water knotted at the top. Inside was —

"A goldfish!" I put the boxes beside the door so I could pick up the plastic bag. The orange fish wiggled, opening and closing her mouth against the side of the bag. I looked around, but there wasn't anyone else in the parking lot. There wasn't a note, either. Just a fish.

I left my boxes behind and burst through the front door, holding the bag with the fish inside. "Ms. Flores! Someone left a goldfish on the front steps!"

"What? Oh, dear!" she said, coming around the front counter. "Poor little thing."

"There wasn't even a note!" I said. "We don't know who left her. Or why. Or how old she is. We don't even know her name. How could anyone do that?"

"Whoever left her should have come in or left us some information." Ms. Flores took the bag from me. "But I'm glad they brought her to us and didn't let her go in a pond or stream. Sometimes people release pets into the wild when they don't want them anymore."

"They just let them *go*?" I asked. "But what if the pet doesn't know how to get food? Won't it die?"

Ms. Flores nodded. "Most times it does die. But even if the pet *does* learn how to get food, it may eat up the food that the native animals need to survive. Goldfish have become problems in some lakes and rivers."

I looked at the fish swimming in a circle.

"But why would someone get a goldfish if they didn't want to take care of it?"

"Sometimes people give fish away as prizes at birthday parties," Ms. Flores said. "Maybe that's what happened. Maybe this fish was a party favor or a prize, but the person who won wasn't ready to give a fish what it needs."

"Just like Merlin's owner wasn't ready to give him everything a ferret needs," I said. "Did he get adopted this week?"

Ms. Flores shook her head. "So he'll be excited to see what you're making for him."

Hattie, one of the waiting-room cats, hopped up on the counter. She had an interested look on her face.

"Oh no you don't, Hattie! This is not a toy for you." Ms. Flores tucked the bag with the fish safely on the bookshelf between some books. "We have a fish tank with a cover in the back room. It'll take me some time to clean it and set it up, though. So we'll put our newest shelter pet right here where the cats can't reach."

From the bookshelf, the goldfish waved her little front fins. She stared at me with her black eyes. Was she scared, wondering why she was alone? She felt like my fish, since I found her.

"It's okay. Don't worry," I told her. "You're in a good place now. We'll take care of you."

It took a few trips to get all the boxes to the workroom. As soon as I opened the door, Ms. Kim said, "Oh, my goodness! Is that you under those boxes, Suzannah? Let me help you with those."

In his pen beside the table, Merlin stood on his back legs to see what was going on. "I knew Merlin would like to join us today," Ms. Kim said. "But we wouldn't get any work done if he was loose. So I brought his pen in here so he can play or nap next to us while we work."

"We're making a surprise for him," I said. "But first, I have another surprise. Someone left a goldfish in a plastic bag on the shelter steps! My mom and I found him."

"Wow!" Matt said. "Good thing you didn't step on her."

"She wasn't there when *we* came!" Allie said, sounding disappointed that she didn't get to find her. "Jada and I would've seen her."

"And there wasn't a note!" I said. "We don't even know her name."

"Well," Ms. Kim said. "That *is* a surprise. After we finish our project for Merlin, we'll go meet her."

I nodded. "Ms. Flores is setting up a tank."

"Suzannah, tell us what we're making," Jada said. "I can't wait anymore!"

"When I read about ferrets, I learned that they like to climb in and out of boxes and tunnels," I said proudly, putting the boxes on the table. "So I thought we could make Merlin a whole town of houses. We can cut out windows and doors for him to climb in and out and peep through. And if you want to, I brought some paper-towel tubes to make tunnels and chimneys."

"This will be so fun!" Matt said.

"What a good idea, Suzannah!" Levi said.

I could feel my face glowing. I might be the youngest, but they liked my project!

"I want this box," said Allie, choosing the biggest one.

Ms. Kim brought out scissors and markers. "Be sure you pull off any tape or labels and check your box for staples or sharp parts. We don't want anything that could hurt him."

"My box will be a school," said Allie. "So Merlin can learn tricks."

"I'm making him a fort," Jada said. "So he can spy on the cats."

"My box is going to be a store," Levi said. "Full of things Merlin likes."

"I'm making him a pizza restaurant with a drive-through window," Matt said. "Except Merlin doesn't drive, so it'll be a run-through window. My restaurant is called Merlin's Munchies!"

I smiled. "And I'm making him a castle. So he can be like the Merlin in King Arthur."

As we cut doors and windows into our boxes, Ms. Kim told us that she'd called all the nearby animal shelters to tell them about Merlin. "Just in case someone comes in hoping to adopt a ferret," she said.

My castle was looking good, but I wanted

towers on top. If I cut some slits in the top, I could push paper-towel tubes up through them. It would be really cute to see Merlin's head popping up in a tower. "Last week at the Make-A-Match-A-Thon, I met a lady who had a ferret that died," I said. "She promised she would tell her friends about Merlin." I grabbed a few tubes to make towers, but one rolled across the table. It dropped off the edge into Merlin's pen. He snatched it happily.

It was another toy for him! Using a big pair of scissors, I made two slits like an *X* in the top of my box for each tower. I fitted the first tower. It looked great! But suddenly, there was a terrible sound from Merlin's

pen. He had the paper-towel tube stuck on his head.

He looked so funny that I couldn't help giggling. But Ms. Kim jumped up so fast, her chair tipped over.

"He's choking!" she cried.

Chapter 8

People Need Help, Too

Merlin was choking. My eyes burned as I tried not to cry. It was all my fault. Ms. Kim grabbed Merlin out of the pen and ripped the paper towel tube away from his head.

Ms. Kim cradled him in her arms.

Was he breathing? *Please be okay*, I wished. *Please be okay.*

Then his tail twitched.

"He's fine," Ms. Kim said as Merlin grabbed her hand in his paws. "But this tube is too small for him. He might've really gotten hurt if we hadn't been here to help him."

I looked down at the table. "It said in the book that ferrets like tunnels, and I saw a photo of a ferret playing with tubes. I thought it would be fun for him. I didn't mean to hurt him."

"The author of the book should've mentioned that some tubes were too small!" said Allie. "Merlin could've died!"

"Maybe we should write to the book's publisher and warn them," Jada said.

"Let's see the picture," Ms. Kim said. She got the ferret book.

I opened it to chapter 6. When I found the photo, my eyes widened. The tube in the picture was a lot bigger than the ones I'd brought.

Allie pointed to the small words near the picture. "It says right here to make sure the ferret can climb all the way through the tube or he could suffocate."

I opened my mouth, but tears were clogging the back of my throat.

"Didn't you read it?" Matt asked.

"I couldn't read it!" I was crying now. "It

was too hard." I looked down at the tabletop, not wanting to see anyone.

"You could've asked *us* for help," I heard Levi say. "I would've read it to you."

"Me, too," Matt said.

"We do so much to help the animals," Ms. Kim said, putting her arm around me. "But sometimes *people* need help. It's always okay to ask, Suzannah."

I glanced up at the pile of paper-towel tubes in the middle of the table. They made my stomach hurt. I had been so excited for us to make the houses, but I'd almost hurt Merlin. "Ms. Kim?" I asked quietly. "Could we read the toy chapter in the ferret book together? I need to make sure everything I said for the quiz is right."

"Of course," she said.

While Ms. Kim and I read the pages together, Jada and Allie removed the paper-towel tubes from all the boxes. Levi collected the extras and put them away in the cupboard where Merlin couldn't get them. Then the other kids decorated their boxes, drawing mailboxes and flower gardens and other fun things.

When we were all finished, Matt said, "Let's put our ferret boxes along the wall. It'll be Merlin's Main Street!"

"I can't wait to see which one he goes to first!" Allie said.

I still felt horrible. Even when you're trying really hard and don't mean to hurt an animal, you can.

Ms. Kim opened the pen door, and Merlin

didn't waste any time. He ran across the room, right for the boxes. He headed toward Matt's pizza restaurant, but then he swerved and ran through the front door of my castle. When he peeked out the window, it looked like he was smiling.

I knelt down beside him. "I'm sorry, Merlin."

But he didn't look mad or upset with me. He made a funny sound. A small smile lifted the corners of my mouth. He was dooking!

Merlin loved his houses. Sometimes he went in and out of the doors. Other times he climbed through the windows. Once, he even leapt into the pizza restaurant using the drive-through window. I loved seeing the boxes wiggle and jiggle while he was inside. Then he'd pop out somewhere and surprise us.

"Merlin is appearing and disappearing again," Matt said.

A knock sounded on the workroom door. Ms. Flores came in, smiling. "Good news! There's a lady in the waiting room who wants to adopt Merlin!"

I jumped up and grabbed the quiz off the table.

Chapter 9

A Home That Needs a Ferret

Ms. Kim tried to pull Merlin out of my castle, but he didn't want to leave it! Finally, she picked up the whole castle with Merlin inside. She put her hand over the doorway. "Suzannah, would you walk beside me and stop him if he tries to get through the windows? I don't want him to fall."

I walked beside Ms. Kim, one hand covering a window, my other hand holding the quiz. But Merlin never peeked out. I felt happy and sad at the same time. Happy that Merlin might get a home today, but sad because I'd miss him.

I spread my fingers to peek through the castle window and make sure he was okay. Merlin was curled up in a far corner inside. I watched his little chest go up and down. "He's napping," I said.

"He's probably dreaming of shiny things," Jada said. "A whole desk drawer full!"

But I thought he was probably dreaming of a new home and someone to love him.

In the waiting room, I noticed the new fish tank on top of the bookcase. Inside, the little goldfish swam back and forth. She looked shimmery as the light shone on her scales. Her tail swished, making her look like she was dancing in the water.

Then I looked at the counter and gasped! Standing next to Ms. Flores was the lady I had met at the Make-A-Match-A-Thon. "This is Mrs. Avery," Ms. Flores said, introducing her.

"Hi again!" I said, grinning.

She smiled back at me. "I know I said I wasn't ready for another ferret, but after meeting Merlin, I just couldn't stop thinking about him. I understand he's still available to be adopted?"

I nodded. "He's asleep in his castle right now. But you can look through the window if you want."

Mrs. Avery came and peered through the castle window. "Such a beautiful boy," she said.

"Our Shelter Pet Squad has created a quiz to make sure Merlin gets a good match," Ms.

Kim said. "If you'd like to adopt him, do you mind if we ask you a few questions?"

Mrs. Avery shook her head. "I don't mind at all."

Ms. Kim read the first question on the ferret quiz. "Have you had a pet ferret before?"

"Yes," said Mrs. Avery. "My ferret, Mitzi, died only a few months ago. I miss her terribly. My house isn't the same without her."

It was Jada's turn next. "What are some good foods and drinks for ferrets?" she asked.

"I always fed Mitzi ferret food that our veterinarian recommended. For drinks, I gave her fresh water every day."

"Is it okay to feed Merlin chocolate?" Jada asked.

Mrs. Avery shook her head. "That would

hurt him. For treats, Mitzi loved eggs. Sometimes I'd cut up bits of meat or fish for her, too."

Jada smiled, handing the questions to Levi. "Will you get mad if Merlin nips you?" he asked.

"No. I'll try to teach him not to," said Mrs. Avery, "but that's how ferrets play."

"Do you have houseplants?" he asked. "Because they like to dig."

"I don't have any big plants inside. But I still have Mitzi's harness and leash," Mrs. Avery said. "She liked to go outside and dig in the garden. Sometimes I took her for walks around the yard. Has Merlin ever been outside?"

"I don't think so," Ms. Kim said. "That would be a fun new adventure for him."

"Will you get mad if Merlin hides your keys?" Levi asked.

Mrs. Avery laughed. "No. I discovered Mitzi's hiding places. I'll learn Merlin's hiding places, too."

I smiled. This was going really well. Mrs. Avery seemed to like Merlin just the way he was.

Allie took the list of questions from Levi. "Where will Merlin live?"

"When he's in his cage, he'll have a habitat with ramps and a little hammock. I use shredded paper for bedding. Does he use a litter box?"

"Yes," Ms. Kim said, taking the quiz paper from Allie. "How do you know when a ferret is sick?"

Mrs. Avery looked like she might cry. "Mitzi stopped eating. When she was awake, she didn't seem like herself. I took her to the vet, but a few days later, she died."

Part of me wanted to stop the quiz so she wouldn't have to talk about Mitzi anymore. But there were still two groups of questions left. "I hope Merlin will make you feel better," I said.

She gave me a small smile. "It's hard to be sad when you have a ferret in the house. They make you laugh every day."

She sure loved ferrets!

"How did you keep Mitzi looking fit, fine, and fabulous?" Matt asked.

"I bathed her in the kitchen sink," Mrs. Avery said. "And she loved to be brushed. I also brushed her teeth every day and clipped her nails when they got long."

Matt gave a thumbs-up and handed the quiz to me.

"What are some good toys for ferrets?" I asked.

"Mitzi liked balls, but her favorite was socks! She would take them out of the laundry basket every chance she had. She also liked to go through tunnels."

"No paper-towel tubes, though!" I said quickly. "A ferret can get hurt with those."

"Really? I didn't know that," said Mrs. Avery. "Thank you for telling me."

Ms. Kim smiled at me. "Even experienced pet owners can learn new things."

"And it's okay to ask for help," I said quietly. "Everybody has to do that sometimes — even if it's hard to tell people you need it."

Ms. Kim opened my castle doors and slid Merlin gently out of the box. He gave a big yawn and blinked a few times as Ms. Kim placed him in Mrs. Avery's arms.

"I didn't think I was ready for another ferret," Mrs. Avery said. "But holding Merlin last Saturday made me realize something. My house just doesn't feel whole without a ferret in it."

"Shelter Pet Squad, what do you think?" asked Ms. Flores. "Does Mrs. Avery pass the test?"

"Yes!" we all said together.

Merlin looked up at Mrs. Avery and dooked. A soft, funny, ferret chuckle.

He thought so, too.

Chapter 10

A Name for a Fish

"I see you've brought your own carrier for Merlin," Ms. Flores said. "But let me find a box to pack his things in. I'm sure he'd like some familiar toys and blankets to start with."

"You could put those in his castle," I said. "As long as nothing falls out of the windows."

"I'd love that," Mrs. Avery said, "but are you sure you want me to take your castle?"

"We also made him a restaurant, a store, a

school, and a fort," Levi said. "Would you like those, too?"

"Yes," said Mrs. Avery. "He could play with a different building every day!"

The other kids rushed down to the work-room to grab their boxes — all except Allie. She started for the hallway but then came over and whispered to me, "I couldn't have read that ferret book when I was in second grade either."

Was she pointing out that she's older than me? And a better reader?

When I stepped back and looked at her face, she wasn't grinning like she was making fun, though. She looked like she was just telling me something.

"Thanks," I said.

As Allie headed down to the workroom to get her box, I called after her, "I'm glad you made Merlin a school." I don't even know why I said that. I just wanted to say something nice, and that was all I could think of. Maybe it was okay, though. Because she called back, "Thanks," as she went into the workroom.

While Mrs. Avery signed the adoption papers, I glanced at the fish tank. Merlin had a new home, but our goldfish still needed us to find her one. She swished her tail, swimming past. It didn't seem fair that we didn't know her name. Or who brought her to the shelter. Or why they left her on the doorstep. But she didn't look sad. She just looked happy to watch everything going on in front of her.

Ms. Kim put Merlin in the pet carrier. Ms. Flores carried a bag of ferret food. We Shelter Pet Squad kids each brought our box out to Mrs. Avery's car.

"Bye, Merlin," Matt said, putting his pizza restaurant in the backseat. "Be careful when you're appearing and disappearing, okay?"

"Be good!" Allie put her school in next. "And don't take things that don't belong to you."

"Have fun digging outdoors in the garden," Jada said.

Our boxes filled up Mrs. Avery's backseat. On the front seat, Merlin pressed his face up against the door of his carrier. Mrs. Avery shut the car doors, almost crying. "It'll be so nice to have a ferret in the house again. I've missed their silly ways."

"Could you send us some photos of Merlin in his new home?" Ms. Kim asked.

Mrs. Avery nodded. "As soon as he's settled, I'll take some pictures."

The car drove away. I reached into my pocket to touch Whiskers, hoping he'd make me feel better. The empty driveway looked so lonely.

"The small animal room will feel very quiet without Merlin," Ms. Kim said.

"The whole shelter will be quiet without Merlin!" Ms. Flores said. "We won't have to keep up with our ferret-proofing now."

She didn't say it like it was a good thing, though. I knew she'd miss Merlin, too.

"At least we won't have to do any fish-proofing," Jada said. "Goldfish can't steal keys or climb into desk drawers."

"That little fish makes me happy whenever I look at her," Ms. Flores said. "I've been thinking that maybe we should keep our newest shelter pet. She can live in the lobby, like Shadow and Hattie."

Keep her? I looked at Ms. Flores to see if she really meant it. She was smiling.

"I think that's a great idea," said Ms. Kim.

"But if she's staying with us, she needs a name. Suzannah, would you like to name her, since you found her?"

My heart jumped. "Yes!" I had named lots of stuffed animals, but never a real one.

The other kids wanted to help me. Levi suggested water names: Splash, Swish, or Bubble.

Jada thought something sparkly would be better: Glitter, Glimmer, or Shiny.

Allie liked color names: Goldie, Tangerine, or Coral.

Matt came up with a list of funny ones: Jaws, Moby Dick, or Nemo.

Those were all good. But I wanted a name that was more than what she looked like. More than where she lived. I wanted a name that was just hers.

As we walked back into the shelter, I looked at the doorstep where I'd found her. She'd been left behind, hoping for a new home.

And, just like that, her name came to me.

A wishing name.

A name full of second chances and promises.

"Her name is Hope," I said.

Chapter 11

Merlin's Second Chance

All week long, I imagined Merlin happy in his new home. Maybe Mrs. Avery had set up our boxes around her living room.

Maybe he was exploring cupboards and trash cans and coat pockets. I hoped Mrs. Avery had ferret-proofed her house really well. Merlin would try to get into everything!

Maybe Mrs. Avery had even put Mitzi's old harness and leash on him and taken him outside. I wondered what he thought of the grass.

On Saturday, I felt sorry we wouldn't have Merlin with us during Shelter Pet Squad. It was always hard to like an animal so much and then watch him leave. But as Mom drove into the parking lot, I knew there were still animals at the shelter that needed us to care for them.

This week, instead of carrying a big book about ferrets, I was bringing a smaller-size book about goldfish to show everyone. I had asked my school librarian to help me find a book that was just the right reading level for me, and I had read every word.

Walking through the door, I saw the other kids were all crowded around the bulletin board.

"Suzannah, come see!" Jada said. "Mrs. Avery sent us photos of Merlin!"

I rushed over and there was Merlin in the castle I'd made.

Wearing his harness outside, playing in a puddle.

Curled up asleep in the sink.

Just his face showing between the couch cushions.

Playing and getting into mischief and just being a ferret.

Mrs. Avery had a huge smile on her face as she held him.

"I bet he's doing a lot of dooking," Allie said.

I nodded. "He has a great home now."

"And you helped him find it, Suzannah," Ms. Kim said. "If you hadn't talked to Mrs. Avery at the Make-A-Match-A-Thon, this might not have happened."

I felt a glow inside. "We all helped, though," I said. "We worked together to find him a home — the *right* home this time."

A home that needed a ferret.

Merlin the Magnificent!

Fast Facts about Ferrets

• Baby ferrets are called kits.

• All kits are born pink. Adult ferrets can have fur that is white, cream, brown, reddish brown, black, silvery gray, and tan. Some ferrets are all white, but most have patterns of colors.

• Ferret kits are born deaf and with their eyes closed. They begin to hear and their eyes open around five or six weeks old.

• The average number of kits in a litter is eight. There can be anywhere from one to eighteen ferrets in a litter, though!

• Ferrets usually live about eight years.

• Ferrets can sleep eighteen to twenty hours a day.

• The word *ferret* comes from the Latin word *furonem*. That means "thief" in Latin.

- A group of ferrets is called a business of ferrets.
- Male ferrets are larger than female ferrets.
- Ferrets are mammals. They are related to weasels.
- Ferrets must eat meat to survive.
- Ferrets have been kept as pets for thousands of years. There are even drawings of animals that look like ferrets wearing leashes on the walls of some Egyptian tombs.

You can learn more about ferrets
at the library and online.

Ways YOU Can Help Shelter Animals in Your Area

• Make a short promotional video about helping shelter animals to show to your class. Maybe your local shelter will want to show it to their supporters or put it on their website, too!

• Ask your local shelter if you can make adoption signs to be hung on the cages of their adoptable animals. Cut a piece of paper into a big speech bubble and then write something inside that the animal might be thinking. Here are a few suggestions to start with:

  • *I'm dreaming of a new home. Maybe yours?*

  • *Best friend available right here. Inquire within!*

  • *I choose you. Will you choose me?*

  • *The people at the shelter are nice, but I wish I had a home of my own.*

• If you ask some questions about each animal, you could make a sign that shows their own personality, too.

> • *Please adopt me. My name is Pete. I like treats, playing with tennis balls, and cuddling. Is there room on your couch for me?*

> • *Hi, I'm Yoda! I'm looking for someone to love and who likes to take walks.*

• Read to the animals. Ask your local shelter if there are some animals who would like you to read to them. Though the animals won't understand the stories, some animals will really enjoy your attention and the sound of your voice.

• Decorate plain bandannas with nontoxic markers or fabric paint for shelter dogs to wear at events. Make them attractive and add a slogan like *Adopt me!*

• Say thank you. Even if you can't volunteer with the animals, shelter workers and volunteers appreciate knowing that people care about the work they are doing. Bring in some homemade cookies or something special to say thank you for all they do to help the animals.

• If your family has adopted a pet from a shelter, take a photo of your pet doing something he loves and write a short update for the shelter, telling how he is doing at your house. Shelter workers love to see glimpses of the animals they've taken care of in their new homes.

• Be sure that your own pets wear ID tags and/or are microchipped so it will be easier for shelters to return your pet to you if he becomes lost. Having identification makes a big difference when a shelter tries to find a lost pet's family.

• Celebrate your pet's birthday by donating a present to your local shelter in your pet's name.

Catnip Critters

To create the cat toys that Suzannah makes in the story, you will need:

- *Plain-colored infant socks (long enough that you can tie a knot in the sock)*
- *Loose catnip (larger pet stores sell this)*
- *Empty toilet-paper tube*
- *Spoon*
- *Nontoxic permanent markers*

1. If the socks you've chosen have rubber grips on the bottom, begin by turning the sock inside out so the grips are on the inside.

2. Open the top of the sock and insert the toilet-paper

tube inside. This will make it easier to add the catnip.

3. Spoon the catnip into the toilet-paper tube so it will fall down into the toe of the sock. About four spoonfuls should fill the toe of an infant sock.

4. Cover the opening with your hand and shake the sock to be sure all the catnip falls down into the toe.

5. Remove the toilet-paper tube. Pinch the sock just above the catnip and knot the sock to seal the catnip inside.

6. Using a nontoxic permanent marker, draw a face and add details to make your toy look like a fish or another animal.

Box Toys for Small Animals

The simplest toys can make your small pet happy. A box makes a fun hideaway for a hamster, mouse, gerbil, guinea pig, ferret, or other small animal. You will need:

- *A plain box big enough for the animal to comfortably fit inside. Twice as big as the animal is a nice, cozy size, but one where he can easily move around.*
- *Safety scissors*
- *Nontoxic markers or nontoxic crayons, edible decorations*

1. Remove all things from the box that could hurt the animal or would be dangerous for him to eat: staples, tape, labels, and stickers. If you aren't sure, remove it.

2. Use scissors to cut doorways and windows and skylights. Be sure all openings are big enough for the animal to crawl through easily.

3. Decorate your house with nontoxic markers or nontoxic crayons or edible decorations.

4. Be sure to supervise your pet playing with his new house to be sure he is safe and happy.

5. When the box becomes damaged or dirty, remove it from the cage.

Is a Ferret a Good Pet for Me?

Ferrets can make fun and lively pets. Bringing a pet into your family is a big decision, though. Here are some questions your family should think about if your family is considering a ferret as a pet.

• Is it legal to have a ferret as a pet where you live? Not all states allow ferrets to be kept as pets.

• Does everyone in your family agree that a ferret would be a good pet for you? Like a dog or a cat, a ferret will become part of your family. Everyone needs to be willing to assist in the care, training, and supervision that a ferret needs.

• Do you have time for a ferret? Ferrets require a lot of care. Every day, you will need to be sure that he has food, water, bedding, a clean cage, and supervised exercise and play time in a safe place outside of his cage. He will also require regular nail clipping, teeth brushing, and baths with ferret shampoo to keep him healthy and smelling nice.

• Do you have enough money for a ferret? In addition to buying the ferret or paying the adoption fee, you will need a cage, dishes for food and water, a litter box, grooming tools and supplies, and toys, as well as regular purchases of food and bedding. You will need to take your ferret to the vet for regular checkups and if he becomes ill.

• Do you have other pets? Ferrets can get along with some dogs and cats, but ferrets should not live in homes with pet mice, guinea pigs, hamsters, gerbils, rats, rabbits, or other small rodents. Your ferret will see those animals as food. Ferrets are also not a good match for a family with pet birds or very small children.

• Do you and your family have the patience to train a ferret? Ferrets can learn to use a litter box and not to nip when playing, but teaching any animal takes time and patience. Ferrets sleep for many hours a day, but when they're awake they have lots of energy and need supervision and your attention.

At my house, we've had many pets over the years. We've never had a ferret, but we had a very special goldfish named Bubble.

Bubble loved people, especially me. When I watched TV, Bubble would swim over to that corner of the tank. If I walked across the room, he'd follow me to the other side. He was excited when I stopped and talked to him.

One day when he was a few years old, he didn't look well. The next day, he was on his back at the bottom of the tank. As I came over, he struggled to turn and see me. Our veterinarian said Bubble had "swim bladder disease." The swim bladder is what keeps a fish upright in the water. Our vet said Bubble would die because he wouldn't be able to eat. That was very hard news to hear.

The next day, I pinched some fish food between my fingers. I reached into the water and put the food against Bubble's mouth. He tried to eat it but couldn't. He couldn't eat the next day, either. On the third day, he ate some. Maybe it was luck or maybe it was because Bubble was trying so hard, but the food went into his mouth.

Bubble surprised everyone. He lived for nine more months. He taught himself to eat and swim upside down! His swimming wasn't graceful like the other fish. He flopped through the water like a rowboat in a storm! It was amazing.

Here are two things that Bubble taught me:

- *Even swimming upside down will get you somewhere.*
- *When people say you can't do something, maybe they're wrong.*

You can learn more about me and see photos of the pets I have today at www.cynthialord.com.

– Cynthia Lord

Be an Honorary Shelter Pet Squad Member!

Pledge:

I promise to be kind and gentle to all animals. I will make sure that any pets in my care are loved, comfortable, safe, and have enough food and water. If I want to approach a pet I don't know, I will ask the owner first. When I am with an animal, I won't only think about what I want. I will think about how that animal might feel and what he wants, too. I will do my part to make the world a better place for animals everywhere.

My name is:

_____

Honorary Shelter Pet Squad Member